Pippi on the Run

by Astrid Lindgren

Pictures by Emily Arnold McCully

Translated from the Swedish

A Trumpet Club Special Edition

Other Books About Pippi Longstocking

Pippi Longstocking
Pippi Goes on Board
Pippi in the South Seas

På rymmen med Pippi Långstrump
(Rabén & Sjögren, Stockholm).

Published by The Trumpet Club
a division of Bantam Doubleday Dell Publishing Group, Inc.
666 Fifth Avenue, New York, New York 10103

ISBN: 0-440-84285-9

This edition published by arrangement with Viking Penguin, a
division of Penguin Books USA Inc.
Printed in the United States of America
September 1990

10 9 8 7 6 5 4 3 2 1
CW

Contents

Here's Pippi

This is Pippi Longstocking, the strongest girl in the world. She must be the kindest, too, and the richest. And maybe she is even the strangest, because she lives in a house without grown-ups. The house is called Villa Villekulla, and Pippi lives there all by herself except for her horse and her monkey, Mr. Nilsson. Her mother and father are not there.

"Of course I have a mother and father," says Pippi. "My papa is Captain Efraim Longstocking. He owns a big ship called the *Hoptoad*, and he sails the Seven Seas. And I also have a mother. Mama is an angel in Heaven. Every now and then she looks down at me through a peephole and says, 'Well done, Pippi,' when I do something good, and, 'No, Pippi,' when I do something bad. But she doesn't worry about what time I go to bed at night or if I keep my house neat and that sort of thing. I don't much like to do housework, you know. Villa Villekulla is very cozy and homelike. At least everybody who comes here thinks so."

Chapter 1

Days at Villa Villekulla

A long time ago Pippi had come riding along and moved into Villa Villekulla with her horse and monkey and a suitcase full of gold pieces. Her father had given her the bag of gold so that she could buy what she needed.

She was singing a song when she first came riding into the village.

> Here comes Pippi Longstocking.
> If you say it fast, it's funny.
> Here comes Pippi Longstocking.
> Oh yes, it's really me.

Yes, it really was Pippi Longstocking. And she has lived in Villa Villekulla ever since.

Pippi has two good friends, Tommy and Annika, who live next door. They come and play every day with Pippi. One of their favorite games is Don't Touch the Floor. They climb all over the kitchen

—on the furniture, on the stove, on the wood-box—everywhere except on the floor. And if there isn't a piece of furniture where it's needed, there's a horse handy to climb on.

Pippi is a good cook. She often asks Tommy and Annika to come over for spaghetti or hot dogs. One day while she was cooking spaghetti, Pippi wondered what she would look like with a beard. After all, she was going to be a pirate when she grew up. She made herself a beard out of spaghetti and trimmed it with a pair of scissors. Then she ate it.

Pippi has sailed around the world with her father and learned to be a good sailor. She can climb in the rigging and do many other things on

a ship. But then Pippi can do almost anything—that's why she's so special.

On her birthday Pippi baked her own birthday cake. She invited Tommy and Annika and the horse and Mr. Nilsson to her party, and she gave Tommy and Annika lots of presents.

"But you're the one who should get the presents, not us," said Tommy and Annika. But it didn't do any good.

"I have a whole chest of drawers full of great birthday presents for you," said Pippi. She had so many because her father had brought her presents from all over the world.

Sometimes Captain Longstocking would come sailing home to see his daughter. He would fire a

salute from the *Hoptoad* when he arrived so that Pippi would know he was home. As soon as they heard the salute, Pippi and Tommy and Annika would rush straight down to the harbor. They'd go aboard the *Hoptoad* and have a wonderful dinner with the Captain. They'd have coconuts and pineapple and bananas and lots of other things that Captain Longstocking had brought with him from the tropics.

Tommy and Annika think it's lots of fun to look around the ship, and Captain Longstocking thinks it's great fun to see how Pippi lives in Villa Villekulla.

Once Captain Longstocking asked Pippi to go away with him on his ship. But Pippi told him she would rather stay in Villa Villekulla.

"Well, maybe it is better for children to live in a house instead of sailing the seas," said Captain Longstocking. "It's clear that your life is much more ordered in Villa Villekulla, and that is probably best for children."

"Absolutely," said Pippi. "Of course it's best for children to live an orderly life—especially if they are allowed to arrange it for themselves."

And Pippi does arrange everything herself. No, she'll never move away from Villa Villekulla.

Tommy and Annika enjoy themselves at home, too, with their mother and father. But guess what? One day they ran away from home. And Pippi went with them.

Chapter 2
Three Runaways

It all began when Annika was angry at her mother, the way you are sometimes. Annika made up her mind to run away, and Tommy decided to go with her.

"Pippi, why don't you run away too?" Tommy asked. He knew that if Pippi came along they would have a much better time.

"Why not?" Pippi answered. "Let's go!"

Pippi had already promised Tommy and Annika's mother that she would go to look after them. She packed a big picnic bag, and away they ran.

"It's really great to have a horse when you're running away," Annika said. "But wait. We forgot Mr. Nilsson."

"I didn't forget him," said Pippi. "I left him home with your mother. He's having a wonderful time."

"Don't you think it would be a good idea to have candy if we're running away?" Tommy asked. "Why don't we buy some just to be safe, Pippi?"

"I'm afraid we can't do that," said Pippi. "I didn't bring any gold pieces with me."

No gold pieces! Why not? Tommy and Annika were puzzled. Pippi had a whole bag full of gold.

"You don't know much about running away, do you?" Pippi asked. "All children who are serious about running away never take money with them."

More than anything in the world Tommy and Annika wanted to prove that they were serious, and so there was no more talk about candy and money.

The weather was beautiful, warm and pleasant, and the sun shone. The horse clip-clopped along at a good pace. After they had ridden for a while, they came across a place where wild strawberries were growing.

"Strawberries are better than candy," Tommy said.

Annika agreed. "And you can thread them on a straw."

The strawberry patch was right by a stream, and the three of them stopped to rest a while.

"This is just the kind of place where people who are running away rest themselves," Pippi said. "They have strawberries for themselves and grass for their horse."

Tommy began to understand how wonderful it

was to run away. He was so happy and excited that he began to hop from stone to stone in the middle of the stream. But suddenly he sat down—*splash*.

Tommy laughed and laughed.

"You're going to laugh yourself to death one of these days," Annika said.

But Pippi just rolled Tommy up in a blanket and hung his clothes on a tree to dry. Then the three of them lay in the grass and gazed up at the blue sky and green trees.

While she was lying in the grass, Pippi made up a summer poem.

> And now I will sing
> That summer is lovely
> And the trees are so fine
> And the earth is so green
> And the flowers are so pretty
> And wild strawberries are so good,
> And the sun is so sunny
> And the water is so wet
> And new freckles I get
> And spotty summer skin
> And that's why I sing
> That summer is mine.

At last they got up and rode on. They wanted to get as far as possible before nighttime.

Chapter 3
A Man Named Conrad

The sun stopped being so sunny. Heavy clouds rolled across the sky, and thunder rumbled in the distance. Annika was afraid.

"Pippi, where are we going to sleep tonight?" she asked anxiously.

"Pooh," said Pippi. "There's probably a wonderful castle around the next bend. The baron who lives there will be delighted to have us stay with him."

But that's not the way it turned out. It began to rain hard. The thunder rumbled louder and louder and came closer and closer. The children had to seek a shelter. The horse didn't like the thunder at all. He was terrified. Suddenly there was a clap of thunder. The frightened horse galloped out of sight, paying no attention to Pippi's shouts.

"What if we never see him again?" Tommy asked.

"Don't worry," Pippi said. "He'll run straight back to Villa Villekulla and be waiting with hot coffee for us when we get back."

There was no castle around the next bend— only an awful old deserted house. Pippi, Tommy, and Annika decided to stay there overnight. Inside, they met a man named Conrad. He was sitting all by himself in one of the empty rooms, playing pretty melodies on a musical saw. He certainly wasn't a baron.

Annika was afraid of him at first. But Conrad wasn't dangerous at all. He was just a small, kind musician and peddler. He traveled around on his bicycle selling Conrad's Gripping Glue, which he showed to them.

"Own invention," he said. "Conrad's Gripping Glue sticks fast. And it glues almost anything. Try it yourself," he said, giving Pippi a can of glue. Pippi tried it. She smeared glue all over her hands and feet and then—would you believe it?—she crawled up the wall like a fly.

"What a glue!" said Pippi. "That can is worth more than a gold piece."

The children opened their picnic bag, and Conrad opened his. They had a small feast. When it's raining and thundering and lightning outside, how cozy and a little exciting it is to sit together on the floor of a deserted house and eat cheese and

tomato sandwiches. At least, everybody who has done it thinks so.

Conrad was a little dirty, especially in his ears. Annika noticed it immediately, and she wanted to wash him right then and there. Conrad was not at all interested in her idea.

"Why are you so eager to wash my ears?" he asked.

Annika thought for a minute. "Because I don't want you to walk around like that, dirty and alone, and—yes, alone."

Pippi laughed. "He won't be any lonelier just because his ears are dirty."

"Anyway, I ride a bicycle. I don't walk," said Conrad.

"That's true. But you can still have clean ears," Annika said, in an understanding tone.

Chapter 4

Pippi Eats Fish Bones and Floats in a Barrel

When they woke up the next morning Conrad had disappeared.

"He was probably afraid he would get his ears washed," Pippi said.

"Pooh. That was Annika's silly idea," Tommy said. "I wonder what's going to happen now?"

The first thing to happen was that they discovered that the road ended at the deserted house. Behind it there were only woods and hills and wild country. Annika wanted to run back and look for another road, but Pippi told her that roads weren't necessary for running away.

"We'll find a way," she said. They went straight into the woods and walked and walked and walked. They were going up all the time. Finally, they stood high on top of a hill that sloped steeply down to a river.

"We've got to turn here," Tommy said. "There's no way down."

"Not so fast," said Pippi. She took a rope from her knapsack. "As long as you've got a rope and gadgets, you can get yourself down from the Himalayas in an emergency."

Tommy and Annika doubted that they could ever get themselves down from the world's highest mountains, no matter how bad the emergency was. But this hill turned out to be easy. Pippi lowered Tommy and Annika carefully. Annika was scared out of her wits, but Tommy laughed.

"You're going to laugh yourself to death one of these days," Annika said.

The river flowed along at the bottom of the hill. There was a mill beside the river, and Tommy wanted to make camp there.

"I'm tired and hungry," he said. "Let's finish the sandwiches." Instead, Pippi built a fire on the riverbank and made two simple fishing rods.

"Keep the skillet warm," she said to Annika. "We're going to get some fish."

"It'll be trout, then," Annika answered.

Trout it was. Two beautiful trout, which they shared as fairly as they could.

Tommy didn't particularly care for fish. "But," he said, "it tastes so much better when you're sitting next to a fire with the smell of smoke and you can hear the river rushing by and the birds in the woods."

"Fish bones also taste especially good when the birds are singing in the woods," Pippi said. With that, she swallowed a fish skeleton—whole.

"That's dangerous. Fish bones are as sharp as needles," Annika said.

"Well, in that case, I've got a pack of needles in my stomach now," Pippi said.

"And a lot of silly ideas in your head," Tommy said. "That's what you've got."

Tommy was right. Because then Pippi had an even sillier idea. There was an old barrel standing by the wall of the mill, and Pippi was delighted when she saw it. "If only we had three barrels," she said. "Then we could all float down the river as easy as anything."

"Thanks a lot," Annika said. "That would really be dangerous. You know that as well as I do."

"You can float over Niagara Falls in a barrel like this," said Pippi. "I know. I've done it myself."

"You're telling lies again, Pippi," Tommy said. He didn't believe that Pippi had floated over Niagara Falls in a barrel.

Pippi crawled into the barrel.

"I'll show you how it's done," she said. "Help push me into the river."

Tommy and Annika shivered. But they almost always did just what Pippi said. And so they closed the lid of the barrel and pushed it to the edge of the river. The barrel rolled down into the water

and drifted away on the current. Tommy and Annika looked on, terrified.

"Come on, Annika," Tommy said. "Let's run along the bank and see where the barrel comes in to land."

They ran along the riverbank as fast as the barrel floated down the river.

"Are you all right, Pippi?" they shouted.

Of course Pippi was all right. The barrel floated faster and faster. Tommy and Annika fell farther and farther behind. Before long they couldn't see the barrel at all.

"She's got to float in to land somewhere," Tommy said. "We just have to keep on following the river and we'll find her."

Pippi sat in the barrel, very happy and content. "It's going faster and faster," she said excitedly to herself. "I can hear the roar of rushing water. I wonder what it is. It sounds almost like Niagara Falls."

Pippi didn't know it, but she was floating closer and closer to a great waterfall. She could hear the roaring grow louder and louder.

"Something has to happen soon," she said. And it did. Crashing and roaring, the barrel was swept over the waterfall.

"Pooh," said Pippi. "It's not exactly Niagara, but it's pretty good."

Chapter 5

Pippi Loses Tommy and Annika

Below the falls the river grew calmer. Soon the barrel floated into the stones along the riverbank and stopped. Pippi climbed out.

"They're pretty speedy, these little barrels," she said. "It's too bad Tommy and Annika couldn't ride with me."

Hey, where were they? Pippi shouted but got no answer.

"Oh, I've probably come too far," she said to herself. She certainly had come too far. She was now far, far away from Tommy and Annika. She had to find them.

Pippi started to run. She shouted and searched, and searched and shouted. She looked next to the river and in the woods. She searched everywhere.

"For goodness' sake," she said to herself. "I've

never seen so little of Tommy and Annika before."
Then she felt sad. The more she searched, the
sadder she felt.

"I'm really silly," she said to herself. "Why did
I have to go and float away in that old barrel?" It
was not a happy ending for a running-away day.

It was evening now, and Pippi had come to a
deserted village. It was in the middle of the woods,
and everybody had moved away long ago.

"I think I'll go to sleep for a while. And then
I'll search again," Pippi said to herself.

She found an old barn, crept in, and lay down
on a pile of old hay. There she fell asleep.

Chapter 6
"We'll Never See Pippi Again!"

Where were Tommy and Annika while Pippi searched? Poor children, they were having an even worse time.

They searched and searched, and shouted and shouted. Annika cried. Oh, how she cried. Then it was evening.

They lay down under a fir tree and tried to sleep a little. But they just lay there and cried and longed to see Pippi again. They wished they had never run away.

"We'll never find her again," Annika said.

Suddenly she jumped up, shrieking. She began to hop around as if her clothes were full of ants. They *were* full of ants.

Tommy laughed for the first time that day.

"Lie down on an anthill yourself," Annika said. "You'll laugh yourself to death."

She definitely did not want to sleep under that fir tree again.

"What about that old barn we saw in the forest?" she asked. "Why don't we go in there? Come on, Tommy, let's go."

They ran to the barn, crept in, and lay down on a pile of old hay.

"This hay feels nice and warm," said Tommy.

It *was* warm, because Pippi had just been lying there a few minutes before. But now she was gone. She had gone out into the woods to look for Tommy and Annika.

"We'll never see Pippi again," Annika said, crying. "Never!"

But they did. Hurray, they did!

The next day they found her, and she found them. All three of them had left the woods and gone into a small village. There, in the middle of the road, they saw one another.

"Pippi!" shouted Tommy and Annika.

"Help!" shouted Pippi. "Help, is it really you?"

"Get out of the way!" shouted a man driving a wagon. He couldn't understand why three children were dancing in the middle of the road, jumping and shouting and laughing and getting in the way of traffic.

"Pippi, do you think a person can be so happy that she could die?" Annika asked.

Pippi thought that maybe—

"I think so," said Tommy. "And if you never eat anything you can die. That's true, too."

He was starving. All three of them were hungry. They had finished the food in the picnic bag long ago, and they had no money.

"We'll have to begin singing sad songs in the street," said Pippi. "People just love sad songs. When I sing the worst one I know, they all cry and give me quarters."

Chapter 7

The Runaways Meet
a Farm Family

 I never knew," Tommy said later, as he was beginning to feel full, "that we could get pancakes just by singing sad songs. It really is strange, if you think about it."

They were eating pancakes, lots of them, while they sat on the wall of a bridge. With each bite they were beginning to feel that running away was better than they had thought.

"But it sure is hard work, just walking and walking," said Annika. She wished they still had the horse.

"Pooh—there are other ways of traveling," said Pippi. "For example, by train. There's one coming now," she said, pointing to a train steaming along the track under the bridge where they were sitting.

All of a sudden Pippi was standing on the bridge wall. "Jump!" she yelled. "Jump!"

And because they almost always did what Pippi told them to do, Tommy and Annika jumped.

"I don't think Mother would like this very much," Annika said, when she was sitting comfortably on the roof of the train.

"Why not?" asked Pippi. "Train travel is the safest."

"I know. But not on the roof. I've never heard of that before."

"Hmm," said Pippi. "In that case let's change to a wagon instead. There's one now," she said, pointing to a hay wagon coming toward them on the road that ran alongside the railroad.

"Jump!" yelled Pippi. "Jump!"

Tommy and Annika jumped. The farmer driving

the hay wagon didn't notice a thing. But when he arrived home at his farm, he saw that he had three children in his load of hay.

"Three nice children," said Pippi. "You ought to be happy."

But the farmer wasn't happy at all. He had a big family of boys himself, and he thought that was enough.

"We don't need any more children here," he said, annoyed.

"You're lucky," Pippi announced, "because we can't stay long. Just overnight. Can we sleep in the hayloft?"

The farmer was even more annoyed.

"He doesn't like us," Annika whispered to Pippi.

"I just don't understand how he can help it," said Pippi.

The farmer's five boys stood in a long row and stared at Pippi, Tommy, and Annika. They were thinking how exciting it was to have new children around. Charlie and Olly and Freddie and Teddy looked really pleased when Pippi jumped down from the hay wagon. But their little brother, Jojo, was the happiest of all.

He trotted up to Pippi and said, "Da!"

Pippi lifted him so that he could stroke the foal standing in the stable.

"So you think we should stay in the hayloft tonight, too, do you? Tell your daddy."

Jojo said, "Da!" again, and his father said it would be all right to stay in the hayloft—but only if they left first thing in the morning.

"Don't worry," Pippi said. "We can't stay here forever just to make you happy."

After the three of them had settled down for the night in the hayloft, Charlie and Olly and Freddie came up with milk and cake. The boys' mother had sent them. She probably knew that children who are running away are almost always hungry.

"Mothers are really wonderful, aren't they?" said Annika. And she began to think about her mother.

Chapter 8
A Lucky Picnic on the Roof

The next morning, Annika got up early and scrubbed the pig. Of course the pig wasn't as clean and neat as Annika was, so it had to be scrubbed.

"Don't you want to be clean?" she asked. The pig wriggled and grunted and finally slipped free of her grasp and scuttled away, scared out of its wits.

Later, Tommy said to Annika, "Wasn't it enough for you to frighten Conrad? Did you have to scare the poor pig to death too?"

"They were both just as dirty," she answered. "So there!"

The farmyard was full of animals. There were horses and cows and pigs and sheep and hens and rabbits and a big, angry bull. There were baby chicks, too, small and soft and yellow and ugly.

Pippi fed them, and lifted one up in her hand to feel how soft it was.

"I like you," she said. "You've got such small, cold feet."

There were some pancakes left in Pippi's knapsack, and she decided to eat breakfast on the roof of the pigsty. It was nice to have a pleasant view while eating breakfast.

As Pippi, Annika, and Tommy were sitting on the roof, Charlie and Olly and Freddie came along, clutching sandwiches. They looked around for Pippi and Annika and Tommy, but they couldn't see them anywhere.

"They've probably gone on their way," said Charlie. He sounded a little sad.

"They could have said good-bye, at least," said Olly.

"What jerks!" said Freddie. "That Pippi was silly."

"Yes, she certainly was silly," Pippi said from the roof. "You're lucky she went away."

Charlie and Olly and Freddie were a little embarrassed, but when they began to laugh Pippi called down to them, "Come on up here and eat your sandwiches." And they did, because they had never tried eating sandwiches on the roof before.

"It's not so crazy, after all," said Freddie.

And so they all sat on the roof of the pigsty and looked out over the farm. They saw the lambs in the field and the cows in the meadow, the cock on top of the manure pile and the angry bull far away in the paddock.

"Here come Dad and Jojo," said Olly. "Dad's going to fix the fence."

"That's his red shirt hanging on the clothesline," said Charlie. "He's going to wear it Sunday."

The children looked out over the farm some more. They saw the foal in the stable and the cat on the kitchen steps and the red shirt on the clothesline and the bull in the paddock and Jojo *in the paddock*. No. It couldn't be! Yes, it was. Jojo was standing on his small baby legs right in front of the bull. His father didn't see him at all. He just kept fixing the fence.

Chapter 9

Pippi Saves Jojo
and Gets a Free Car

The bull!" shouted Pippi. "Look at the bull!" She jumped straight off the roof.

"Da!" said Jojo to the bull, trying to be friendly. But it didn't help. The bull didn't want any babies in the paddock. He snorted. Then he lowered his head and got set to charge.

Just then Pippi came on the scene.

"Do you know how they fight bulls in Spain?" she asked.

The bull couldn't care less about what they did in Spain. He just wanted the children out of his paddock—especially Pippi.

"Here's what they do," she said. She waved the red shirt in front of the bull's angry eyes. While Pippi was showing the bull how bullfighters fight bulls in Spain, Jojo's father came running. He lifted his son over the fence to safety.

"Hurray for Pippi!" shouted Tommy and Annika. All the children stood in a long row outside the fence and watched Pippi dance in front of the bull while he tried his best to hook her with his horns.

"Aren't you afraid?" Charlie asked. "That bull can kill her."

"Ha-ha," said Tommy. "Pippi is the strongest girl in the world. Didn't you know that?"

Pippi probably was the strongest girl in the world. The bull didn't know that, of course. Not

to begin with. But after he tried one hundred and eighteen times to stick his horns into Pippi, he understood it. Suddenly, he was very tired.

"So there, my little friend," said Pippi. "Go home and rest now. And think how lucky you are not to be a bull in Spain!"

The bull walked away, turning his head once to give Pippi a long, weary look.

Guess—was Jojo's father happy that Pippi had rescued his little boy from the bull? He was even happier when he saw Pippi jump over the paddock fence and land on her nose in the mud.

"He almost laughed himself to death," Annika said afterward.

But they all laughed together, and Pippi laughed the hardest.

"Too bad the bull didn't see it," she said. "He would have enjoyed it."

The farmer laughed so hard because he was so happy. Now he didn't want Pippi to leave.

"You saved my son's life. You should be rewarded."

"Oh, I do things like that for free," said Pippi.

She didn't want to talk about it any more. To change the subject, she pointed to an old, broken-down car that looked interesting. "What a nice car," she said.

"Yes," said the farmer. "It's a nice car all right. It's a wreck. Completely worn out. It won't go an inch. Do you want it?" He laughed at the idea.

"Do you really mean I can have it?" Pippi said, excited.

"Sure, if it's any good to you. But since you can't take it away from here, you'll have to come back to play with it."

Can't take it away! The farmer didn't know Pippi. Two hours and thirteen minutes later the car was repaired.

"Giddyap, off we go!" shouted Pippi when the car was fixed. Do you know how she fixed the car? With Conrad's Gripping Glue. Didn't he say it would stick to anything?

"He was absolutely right," Pippi said. "It's excellent glue, and if you mix it with water, it's ten times stronger than gasoline," she said, while filling up the tank. When the engine had started, it putt-putted merrily away.

"What a great putt-putt noise," said Annika.

They got ready to leave. Just as they drove out of the gate, the farmer saw them, and he began to jump and shout.

"Stop!" he yelled. "Children aren't supposed to drive cars."

"Of course they're not," said Tommy. "But this is Pippi Longstocking, remember?"

Chapter 10

Good-bye, Car;
Good-bye, Clothes

The farmer and his sons stood in a long row and listened to the putt-putt of the motor grow fainter and fainter as the old car went farther and farther away.

"Hey, listen to the wind rustling the leaves," shouted Pippi. "What a great car!"

Of course the wind always rustles the leaves in trees, and it probably was a great car. But it had one flaw: no brakes. Pippi and Tommy and Annika rushed along in the car. The people and animals who saw them turned pale. And then—believe it or not—the car began to fly.

"If we're still alive when this is over, will I be surprised," said Annika to herself.

The next second the car landed—with a splash. A splash, because it landed in a lake. Luckily they were close to the shore.

"Oh-ho," said Pippi. "With brakes like that you can forget about giving me a lift again," she said to the car. "Good-bye."

Pippi looked around her contentedly. "We're in luck," she said. "We can swim here."

Pippi always went swimming with her clothes on. "I can wash them out at the same time. It's practical," she said.

"I'll never be that practical," Annika said. She and Tommy undressed and laid their clothes on a rock.

Annika took a bar of soap from the knapsack.

"One of these days they're going to make you chief of the Board of Health," Pippi said, as Annika began to scrub Tommy. She was determined. Conrad and the pig—well, they were different. But her brother had to be washed clean. At least he wouldn't be as squirmy as the pig.

"That's enough," said Tommy. "I'm clean now, so you can rest, Annika."

They swam and dived and played in the water for a long, long time. At last Pippi said, "On your mark, get set, go. And when I say go, I mean go. Remember, we don't have a car anymore."

Suddenly Annika gave a yell. "Our clothes! They're gone!"

"Who on earth could have taken them?" Tommy asked. But then he saw who had taken them, and he fell down laughing. He laughed so

loud that the cow in the field stopped chewing his shirt and stared.

"Now you know why I take a bath with my clothes on," said Pippi. "As long as there are hungry cows anywhere, I will swim with my clothes on. All seven petticoats, too!"

The cow had eaten all of Tommy's and Annika's clothes.

Annika began to cry. "Now what will we do? We can't run away naked."

Pippi thought for a while. "We'll just have to sing sad songs again," she said at last.

"We can't go around singing sad songs dressed like this," said Annika. "We'll get laughed at."

"Let them laugh," said Pippi.

They found some old gunnysacks and made clothes for Tommy and Annika. "Well, I'm glad we don't have to run away naked," said Annika. "But I do wish we had decent clothes. Clothes that people wouldn't laugh at."

Chapter 11
Pippi's Sad Song Doesn't Work

When they came to a small town, almost all the children grinned at them as they went by. There were lots of children because it was market day.

"Hello," said a boy. He pointed at Tommy and Annika. "What are they supposed to be?"

"Two lords from Egypt," said Pippi. "But you won't understand. Wait until you're older."

Pippi began to realize that they needed a really sad song because of those clothes. Otherwise people would not part with their money. She decided to make up a sad song.

"This is called 'The Really Sad Song About Tommy and Annika,'" Pippi said. "It's really about you two. People will sniffle so that the whole town will hear—just because they take pity on you."

"Pooh," said Tommy. "There's no reason for anyone to pity us. Sing that we are brave and courageous even if things are against us and we don't have decent clothes. Sing something like that!"

"I'll try to fit it all in," said Pippi. She thought hard for a long time. At last she had the song ready.

"Now, when I come to the chorus," she said, "you begin to dance your heart out. Otherwise people won't realize how you stay in a good mood when things are going against you—or whatever it was that you said, Tommy."

Tommy and Annika promised to dance their hearts out. They went to the village square, and Pippi tuned her vocal chords and began to sing:

See these poor children; they have no clothes;
They have no father;
They have no mother;
And for fifteen days they haven't seen food.
Can you imagine? They still feel good.

Lira lopa lura glam and turaley
And ick ack ock and liver paté
And collar studs and trousers and hula hula hey
And lira lopa lura and okey dokey day.

All day long these poor kids get punished
And every night it's smacks
And always nagging and shouts,
And all they have to play with is an empty
    bottle
And Grandma isn't kind at all,
But they sing just the same and they have a
    ball.

Lira lopa lura glam and turaley
And ick ack ock and liver paté
And collar studs and trousers and hula hula hey
And lira lopa lura and okey dokey day.

And these poor children have a tummy ache
And they can hardly walk.
Their legs are worn out and then
They have ugly rashes on their bodies, and
    when
They have hiccups—both of them—
They sing happily and laugh and grin.

Lira lopa lura glam and turaley
And ick ack ock and liver paté
And collar studs and trousers and hula hula hey
And lira lopa lura and okey dokey day.

They waited for the money to roll in. But all
they got was a nickel and two pennies.

"I've never met such stingy people before," said Pippi.

Then Annika remembered that it was market day. "They don't want to hear sad songs," she said.

Pippi thought for a while. "We need something stronger," she said. "I've got it!"

Chapter 12

Pippilotta, the Fantastic Tightrope Dancer

U p till then it had been a peaceful and quiet market day in that small town. All of a sudden the peace and quiet were shattered. Someone started to shout so that everyone could hear. The shouting echoed among the houses.

"Come and see Pippilotta, the fantastic tightrope dancer, world famous throughout all of Sweden!"

The people began to giggle. They had seen who was shouting high up on the tower of the town hall. It was a little red-haired girl. Heavens—was she going to walk on that tightrope? She wasn't going to be that foolish. Yes, she was! Goodness gracious. She might fall! Where are the police? Can't anyone stop her? No, no one could stop Pippi now.

"Hola-hop!" she shouted. She ran out on the tightrope. Several people in the crowd began to feel dizzy. Annika felt her stomach fall, and had only enough nerve to open one eye.

"I know you're a little surprised," Pippi shouted. She scratched her right ear with her left foot. "But you should have seen my grandmother!" she called, hanging with the rope under the backs of her knees. "She walked the tightrope so long she had blisters on her feet!"

While Pippi hung from the tightrope, telling the story about her grandmother, Tommy and Annika wandered among the crowd and collected money in tin cans.

"It costs a dime to look," said Tommy.

"Shut your eyes if you don't want to pay," said Annika.

Of course, everyone was happy to pay for the privilege of seeing the great tightrope artist Pippi-lotta. The tin cans were soon full.

Just then the village policeman came along. When he saw Pippi, he turned pale. "Come down, little girl, come down!" he shouted.

He began to ask Tommy and Annika questions. He soon discovered that the three of them were running away. And they were making a spectacle in *his* town.

"Hola-hop!" shouted Pippi on the tightrope. "This is the end of the show. Grandma may have been a professional tightrope walker, but I'm not."

When she came down, Pippi took Tommy and Annika to a store, and with the money they had collected they bought new T-shirts and jeans.

"Now I feel human again," said Annika.

"Yes," said Pippi. "Just don't forget to run when you see a cow."

As they came out of the store they saw the policeman. He was waiting for them.

"My dear children," he said. "Unfortunately, I must take you to the police station."

Chapter 13

Everyone Who Runs Away Comes Home

He was a kind and generous policeman. He gave them sandwiches and milk at the station and a bag of candy for dessert.

"You realize that I'll have to talk to your parents about this," he said to Pippi.

"That might be difficult," said Pippi. "But you could try."

"I don't think they would like to have their little girl running away and walking on a tightrope and maybe falling down."

"You can always ask them," said Pippi.

"I will," he said. "First, I have to lock you up so that you won't run away. We'll meet again soon."

"I don't think we will," said Pippi. But the policeman had already gone and didn't hear her.

"Too bad," said Pippi. "He was a very kind policeman."

The window had iron bars on it. Pippi had no

trouble breaking them up. It took about two minutes.

"I'll send a gold piece to the policeman when I get home," she said. "I've really wrecked the station for him."

They crept out of the prison cell.

Wait—what had Pippi said? "When I get home."

Suddenly Annika felt a great longing to be home again. Oh, how she missed her mother and father and her own soft bed.

"Pippi, I don't want to run away anymore," Annika said. Tommy said the same. They both looked anxiously at Pippi and wondered what she would say.

"Hola-hop," said Pippi. "Everyone who runs away comes home in the end."

The road home was very, very long. And it began to rain.

"I'm cold and hungry and soaking wet. My feet hurt, too," said Tommy. "Why did we ever run away?"

"So that it would be nice to come home," Pippi answered.

Then she said something wonderful: "Look, there's my horse!" And so it was. The horse whinnied happily when he saw Pippi.

"Here, boy," said Pippi. "Did you know I was going home? You couldn't have come at a better time."

Chapter 14
The Very Best House of All

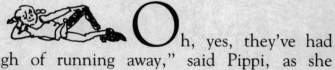Oh, yes, they've had enough of running away," said Pippi, as she handed Tommy and Annika over to their parents. They hugged one another and said how happy they were to be home.

"And aren't you glad that old Pippi has come home?" she asked Mr. Nilsson when he jumped up onto her shoulder.

"Pippi, won't you stay and have dinner with us?" asked Tommy and Annika's mother.

"No, I have to get home with my animals," said Pippi. "Throw me a hot dog."

She rode home to Villa Villekulla. Her red

braids looked a little sad in the rain, but otherwise everything was fine.

Tommy and Annika's parents were good and surprised when they saw their children's new clothes.

"A cow ate up the old ones," said Tommy.

"A cow?" shouted their mother. "Were you children in danger?"

"Danger?" Tommy and Annika thought for a while.

"No, not really," said Tommy.

Tommy and Annika just wanted to lie down and sleep.

"Oh, my little pillow, how soft you are," said Annika when she was lying in bed. "It's too bad Pippi doesn't have a mommy and daddy."

"Let's look and see what she's doing," said Tommy.

They could see straight into Pippi's kitchen from their window. She never closed the curtains.

"Look, there she is, sitting," said Tommy. "I wish it were morning so that we could go over there."

"It'll be tomorrow soon, and then we'll go to Pippi's, tomorrow and every day."

Tommy and Annika waved to Pippi, but she didn't see them or hear their shouting either. "Thanks, Pippi, for running away with us."

And was Pippi happy to be home again?

You bet she was!

Mr. Nilsson was happy, too, that Pippi had come home.

"We live in the very best house of all," said Pippi. "We live in Villa Villekulla."

THE END

About the Author

Astrid Lindgren lives in Stockholm, Sweden. Her books about Pippi Longstocking have been translated into many languages. She has won honors for her work, including the Hans Christian Andersen medal, which is the highest international award for children's literature.